Uncle John's
CITY GARDEN

Uncle John's CITY GARDEN

by
BERNETTE G. FORD

Illustrated by
FRANK MORRISON

OKRA

HOLIDAY HOUSE · NEW YORK

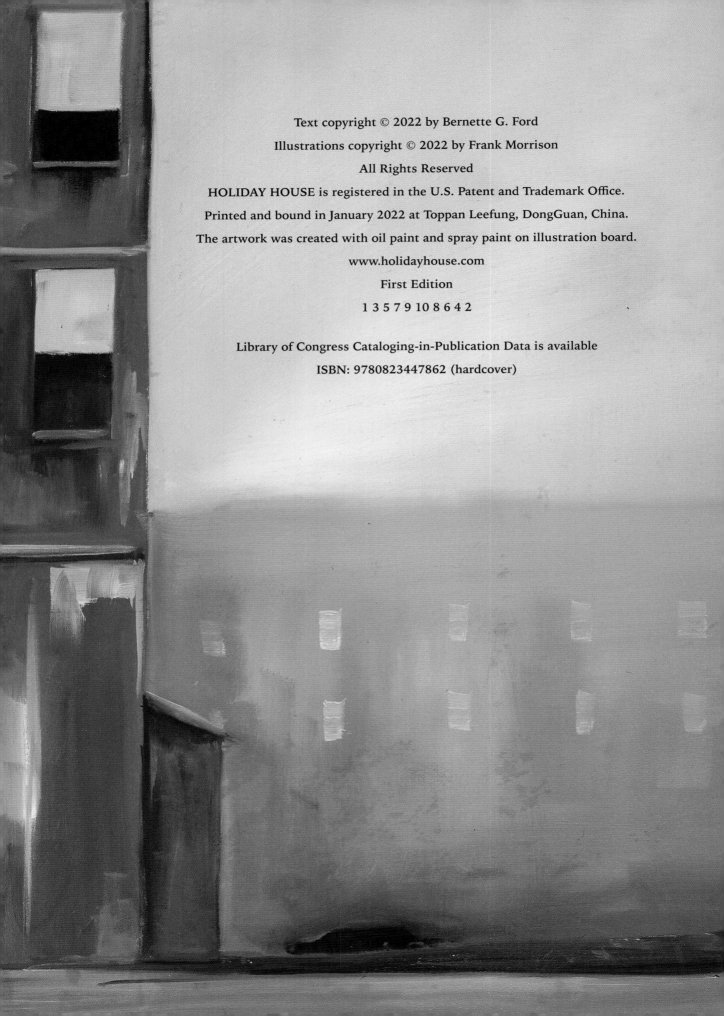

HOLIDAY HOUSE is registered in the U.S. Patent and Trademark Office.

Printed and bound in January 2022 at Toppan Leefung, DongGuan, China.

The artwork was created with oil paint and spray paint on illustration board.

www.holidayhouse.com

First Edition

1 3 5 7 9 10 8 6 4 2

Library of Congress Cataloging-in-Publication Data is available

ISBN: 9780823447862 (hardcover)

To Orian, Gramma's joy!
—B.G.F.

To my first grandson, Miro.
Grandpop loves you, man!
—F.M.

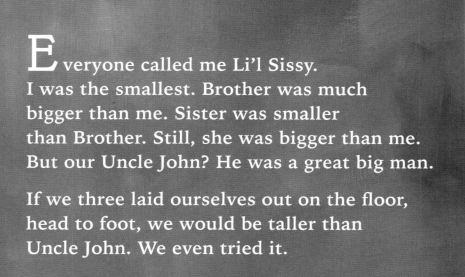

Everyone called me Li'l Sissy.
I was the smallest. Brother was much
bigger than me. Sister was smaller
than Brother. Still, she was bigger than me.
But our Uncle John? He was a great big man.

If we three laid ourselves out on the floor,
head to foot, we would be taller than
Uncle John. We even tried it.

The first summer we worked in Uncle John's Garden, we thought it was the biggest garden in the city. When we looked up and up and up, all around us were tall, tall buildings—all brick, all the same. Right in the middle of the projects was "the garden." That's what everyone called it.

We stood at the top of the little dirt hill and looked down at the garden. There were no plants yet—just fresh-raked dirt.

We jumped off the hill to the garden below. Each of us got to pick our own packs of seeds. Brother chose corn and lima beans. Sister chose tomatoes and onions. I chose okra.

When we told Mother, she laughed. She said we were growing succotash. I was glad. I love succotash!

Uncle John had already done the digging and raking.
He showed us the rows we were each going to plant.
He wrote on some cards and stuck them on sticks.

I had one long row for my okra. Sister had two rows, for tomatoes and onions. Brother had three rows—two for corn and one for lima beans. Uncle John had lots and lots of rows.

Uncle John gave each of us a shovel. My shovel had a short, little-bitty handle. Sister's shovel had a handle longer than mine. Brother's shovel was even longer, but not as long as Uncle John's. His was as tall as Brother.

While Uncle made little hills with his shovel, we used ours to dig little holes in the hills. Then we dropped our seeds into the holes.

After we finished planting, Uncle John brought the hose. He helped us gently water our rows.

We were tired and thirsty, hot and sweaty, but we felt good. We could hardly wait to see our garden grow.

As the weeks passed, Mother took us to work in the garden almost every day. We pulled weeds and picked off bugs and watered.

Our plants had grown a little bit bigger. First just tiny seedlings, not even up to my shins.

Then the shoots grew a little more. . . .
One day my okra was up to my knees. . . .
A while later, my plants would be up to my waist.
The okra would someday be almost as tall as me,
with beautiful flowers! I thought the okra pods
would never appear.

More time passed. Then one day, as we were about
to leave for the garden, the sky grew dark.
The clouds were thick and black.
Thunder roared and lightning flashed and
down, down, down the rain poured.
Then wind began to blow.
We couldn't go.

What would happen to our garden in this storm?
Would my okra ever grow as tall as me?
Mother said our plants would come to
no harm. But we didn't think so.
Boom, boom, crack, bang!
How could anything grow?

During the night, the storm stopped. Next day
the garden smelled fresh and clean. Everything
was all pretty and green. And our plants had grown.

Some were the same size as Sister. Brother's corn
was almost as tall as Uncle John. The tomato plants
were as tall as me. One of the tomatoes was so big
I needed two hands to hold it.

We were so happy we couldn't help but jump up
and down and hoot and holler!

Uncle John showed us how to pick our crops.
He gave us bags to put our vegetables in. Brother
had a big one for his corn and lima beans. Sister's
bag was not as big as his. My bag was little, like me.
We picked a lot of vegetables. But every day when
we came back, the garden had grown some more.

Summer was almost over. Soon we would have to go back to school. All our cousins and uncles and aunts came to the garden for a big barbeque.

Uncle had spread out tables—a long one for our cousins, a shorter one for the teenagers, and the shortest one for Mother and the other grown-ups.

Uncle John cooked chicken and ribs and burgers. He even cooked up some succotash. Best succotash I ever tasted!

At the end we picked and wrapped up vegetables in big brown paper bundles. We had grown so much food, everyone got to take some of our garden home with them.

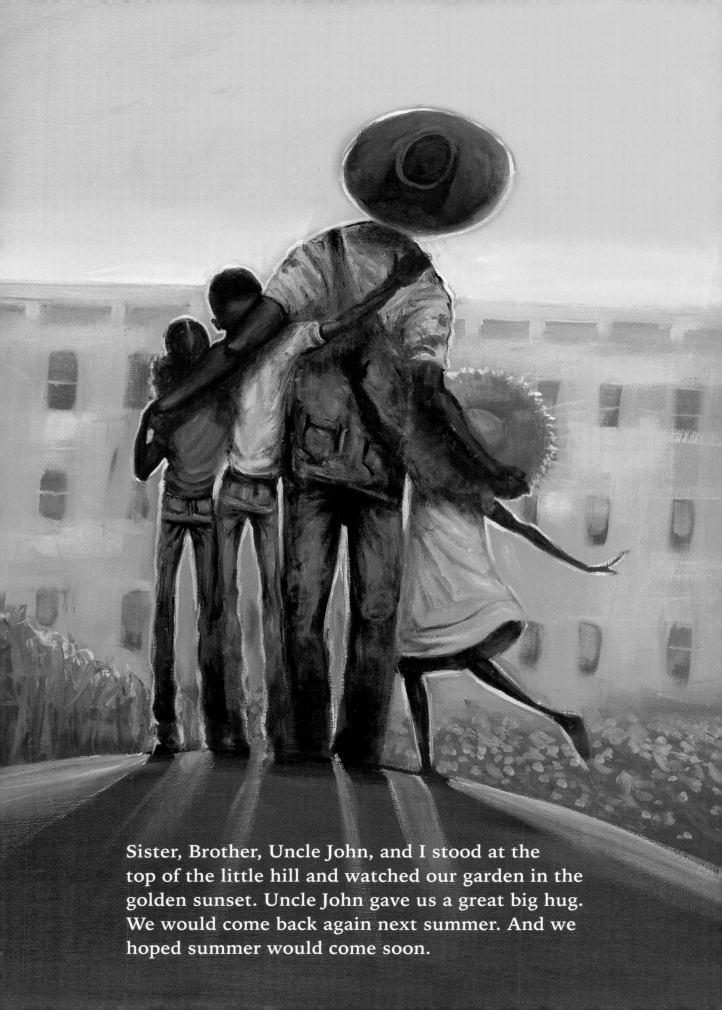

Sister, Brother, Uncle John, and I stood at the top of the little hill and watched our garden in the golden sunset. Uncle John gave us a great big hug. We would come back again next summer. And we hoped summer would come soon.

AUTHOR'S NOTE

This is an "almost" true story. When I was a little girl in the 1950s, my Uncle John lived in the projects in Canarsie, in Brooklyn, NY. He and my mother were the youngest of seven surviving siblings born on a plantation in Louisiana where their father worked and was "in charge" of the other Black laborers on the plantation. All the children had to work in the fields. Everyone eventually left the plantation as young adults, but Mother and John never stopped loving to grow gardens full of food and flowers. When the building of the projects was ended, the huge, deep excavation for the final building was left empty. Uncle John got permission from the City to grow a garden down in that hole. I visited "the garden" often as a child but I never got to spend a whole summer working in it. I wished I could have, and now, in this story, I have.

This material is based upon work supported in part by the TERC* under a grant from the Heising-Simons Foundation

*TERC (Cambridge, MA), a non-profit research and development organization, the developers of the "Investigations in Numbers, Data, and Space" mathematics curriculum

SUCCOTASH

(Adult supervision required.)

❧ Ingredients ❧

1 tablespoon olive oil

½ cup fresh or frozen cut okra
(or 1 small fresh zucchini, diced)

1 cup chopped onion

1 garlic clove, finely chopped

1 14.5-ounce can diced tomatoes
with their juice

½ cup water

16-ounce package frozen corn kernels
(approximately 4 cups)

16-ounce package frozen baby lima beans
(approximately 3 ½ cups)

¼ cup chopped fresh basil
(approximately 12 leaves)

❧ Directions ❧

1. Heat 1 tablespoon olive oil in a skillet or 3-quart saucepan over medium heat.

2. Add okra. Cook until no longer slimy, approximately 10 to 12 minutes.
(Or add zucchini and cook for approximately 5 minutes, stirring occasionally.)

3. Add onion and garlic until onion is soft (approximately 5 minutes),
stirring occasionally.

4. Add tomatoes in their juice and water. Cook for 10 minutes at a slow
simmer, adjusting heat if necessary and stirring occasionally.

5. Add corn and lima beans. When corn and lima beans are thawed,
bring to a slow simmer, adjusting heat if necessary, and cook covered
for 8 to 10 minutes or until done. (Refer to frozen food packages.)

6. Turn off heat and add basil.

Serves 10.

Feel free to adjust
proportions of
vegetables to your
liking or substitute
other vegetables.

Bernette G. Ford is the co-author of the groundbreaking bestseller *Bright Eyes, Brown Skin*. She is also author of the bestselling Ballet Kitty series, *No More Diapers for Ducky*, and for Holiday House, *First Snow*. A publishing pioneer, she was the first African American vice president of children's books at a major publisher. *Uncle John's City Garden* was inspired by her uncle's urban garden in Brooklyn, New York.

Before becoming a children's book illustrator, Frank Morrison was a graffiti artist and break-dancer. While on tour in Europe, he visited the Louvre, where paintings by the masters inspired him to take his art in a new direction. Frank has won a Coretta Scott King-John Steptoe Award, a Coretta Scott King Illustrator Honor, a Coretta Scott King Illustrator Award, an NAACP Image Award, and a Society of Illustrators Original Art Silver Medal. He lives in Georgia.